Dog Days

For Margaret, Ruth, and Anthony

A Doubleday Book for Young Readers
Published by
Random House Children's Books
a division of
Random House, Inc.
1540 Broadway
New York, New York 10036

DOUBLEDAY and the anchor with dolphin colophon are registered trademarks of
Random House, Inc.

Visit us on the Web! www.randomhouse.com/kids
Educators and librarians, for a variety of teaching tools, visit us at www.randomhouse.com/teachers

Library of Congress Cataloging-in-Publication Data
Harvey, Amanda.
    Dog Days / written and illustrated by Amanda Harvey.
        p. cm.
    "A Doubleday book for young readers."
Summary: When a new kitten joins the family, Otis the dog feels neglected and must learn to adjust.
    ISBN 0-385-74621-0 (trade)   ISBN 0-385-90860-1 (lib. binding)
    [1. Dogs—Fiction. 2. Cats—Fiction.] I. Title.
PZ7.H26745 Dm 2003
    [E]—dc21   2002007322

The text of this book is set in 19-point Truesdell.
Printed in the United States of America
January 2003
10 9 8 7 6 5 4 3 2 1

Dog Days

Amanda Harvey

A Doubleday Book for Young Readers

This morning a most unexpected thing happened.

Lucy and her little sister came home with a kitten.
They wouldn't stop fussing over this meowing fluff ball.

But what did they want a kitten for? They had me!

The kitten this. The kitten that. I was forgotten.
I did not get my breakfast.

Or my bed shaken out.

Or my fur brushed.

And even though I made a huge amount of noise,
no one noticed when I went out.

I decided to roam the streets.

Doing the things I'm not normally allowed to do.
It was a good morning.

But when the day got hot,
being on my own wasn't much fun anymore.

So I sat under a tree and watched other dogs go by.

Did they have to share their home with a kitten? I wondered.

Were their bellies grumbling?
Were their mouths dry? Somehow I didn't think so.

It was time to take action.
It was time to sniff out a new family.

This one looked like fun.

Then again, perhaps that one could use a protector.

Better yet, I was sure of getting my fur brushed
with the clan over there . . . and maybe a tartan coat too!

Or an absolutely huge breakfast with this bunch.

Soon I noticed that we were passing Max's house.
I bounced right in . . .

. . . just in time for a small snack.

This was the place to be.

But as night came on, I was filled with thoughts of Lucy.

What had she done all day? Was she managing without me?
Who would she read her book to?

I kissed Max goodnight

and ran home.

The new kitten was asleep.
Lucy shook out my blanket.

Then she read *Great Dogs in History* (my favorite). "But you're the greatest dog of all, Otis," Lucy said. "You're my best friend."

Lucy fell asleep. I was wide awake. Tomorrow I was going to show the kitten how I open the fridge door with my paw.